Over a Fence

by

Ruth J. Hartman

Published by esKape Press
www.eskapepress.com

This is a work of fiction. Names, places, characters, and events are fictitious in every regard. Any similarities to actual events and/or persons, living or dead, are purely coincidental. Any trademarks, service marks, product names, or named features are the property of their respective owners and are used for reference only and not an implied endorsement.

Except for review purposes, the reproduction and distribution of this book in whole or part, electronically or mechanically, without the written permission of the publisher is unlawful piracy and theft of the author's intellectual property. If you would like to use material from the book, other than for review purposes, please obtain written permission first by contacting the publisher at eskapepress@eskapepress.com.

Thank you for your support of the author's rights as provided for in the U.S. Copyright Act of 1976.

For subsidiary rights, foreign and domestic, please contact the publisher at eskapepress@eskapepress.com

If you'd like to know about new releases and giveaways, please sign up for our mailing list by visiting eskapepress.com and completing the form on the sidebar. We will never sell or share your information.

All Rights Reserved
Copyright © 2015 RUTH J. HARTMAN
ISBN-10: 1518702902
ISBN-13: 9781518702907
Cover Art Design by For the Muse Design

Other titles by Ruth J. Hartman

Historical Romance

His Lady Peregrin
A Courtship for Cecilia
The Unwanted Earl
Love Birds of Regent's Park
The Matchmakers
Romancing the Dustman's Daughter
Romance at the Royal Menagerie
Rescued by a Duke
Time for a Duke
Maid for Romance

Contemporary Romance

Flossophy of Grace
Pillow Talk
Cats and Cowboys
Better Than Catnip
Purrfect Voyage
Grin and Barrett
Mind of a Stranger
Waylaid

Memoir

Life in Mental Chains

Children's Book

Murphy in the Paw-Paw Patch

Dedication

To my husband Garry—my crush that's held from age 18 to marriage of 33 years. I love you!

CHAPTER ONE
Cora

I LUGGED MY heavy suitcase up the front steps of my parents' house. The luggage landed with a thud. I yelped, barely jumping out of the way before my bare toes were smashed. It had been so hot in my non-air-conditioned car that I'd ditched my shoes two hours earlier on the long drive from Michigan to Indiana. How strange to be there at the house alone. But when Dad asked if I wanted to housesit for a year while he oversaw a building project in Florida, who was I to turn it down?

I'm not stupid, after all.

Something soft brushed my bare ankle. "Hey, Chubbs." I reached down to pick up my gargantuan one-year-old cat, his long orange fur sticking to the sweat on my arms. "So what you do think of the house?"

Chubbs pawed at my arm and leaped down, racing across the white painted boards of the porch and around the side of the house. Guess he was tired of being cooped up in the hot car too.

I said I was alone, but I wasn't, really. Chubbs was good company. I'd found him outside my college apartment six months earlier. He'd decided my home was his home and that was that. Still, someone of the male, human variety wouldn't be bad to have for company, either.

Chubbs screamed from the back of the house. I ran, following the route he'd taken. When I reached the backyard, there was no sign of him. What in the world? Another yowl came from the direction of the neighbor's. Drew Dunkirk's yard.

I ran to a fence I'd never seen before. When had the Dunkirks built it? I peered over the top. A huge shaggy brown dog had my cat cornered under a patio table.

Uh-oh.

Finding a foothold on a lower cross-board, I pushed up and climbed over the fence. Pain shot through me as my foot got wedged between two pointed boards. The rest of me toppled toward the ground.

Hanging upside down from a neighbor's fence wasn't the best place to be. Ever. *Isn't this perfect?* Maybe I could disengage myself before anyone saw—

"Need some help, there?" came from somewhere around my toes.

With all my blood rushing to my head anyway, my blush might not be noticeable. My thoughts clouded, and I shook my head to clear it but that didn't help. I lifted my chin from my view of the Dunkirk's grass and saw tennis shoes. Hopefully it was Mr. Dunkirk and not his wife. I'd pity any woman who had such a deep voice and that much hair on her ankles.

I waved my arm in the general direction of my feet. "I um...yeah. I'm sorta stuck."

"I can see that." He chuckled. Why was he laughing at me? A warm hand grasped my foot and gave a tug. Before I could tumble the rest of the way into the grass, I was lifted by my waist and set on my feet.

I turned to thank Mr. Dunkirk. But it wasn't him.

Oh no. "Hey, Drew."

"Hey yourself, Cora. Saw you park in your parents' drive a few minutes ago."

I smoothed down my shirt, which had risen dangerously close to my breasts when I'd been inverted. How much had he seen? "Thanks for—"

"Saving you?"

I nodded. How was he even better looking now than he'd been in high school? It had been four years since I'd seen him at our graduation. His dark eyes appeared browner and his sandy hair had deepened in color to a light brown. And his build. Oh my word. I didn't remember him having quite so many muscles before.

Not that I'd been looking or anything.

Drew crossed his arms. "Nice to see you again. Uh, what were you doing hanging from my fence?"

His fence? Where were his parents?

I was slightly dazed from the whole hanging upside down thing. It took me a few seconds to remember exactly what I had been doing there. Taking a nap? Bird watching? *No...*

I gasped. "Chubbs!"

He raised his eyebrows. "Did you call me *chubs*? I know I've put on weight since high school, but honestly—"

"No. My cat." I pointed behind Drew to the huge dog that sat staring at Chubbs.

He turned. "Oh. You have a cat?"

What did that mean? "Yeah. I always had one growing up. Did you forget that?"

"Guess I was hoping you'd outgrown it."

"Outgrown..." Why would anyone want to? I frowned at him and headed across the yard toward the animals. Halfway there, my bare foot sunk down in a hot stinking pile of dog— "Ewwww!" I lifted my foot behind me like a flamingo, gave a hard shake, and wiped my foot on the grass, but some of the revolting substance refused to dislodge. "Get it *off!*" I pointed but refused to get my hand anywhere near the contamination.

Drew let out a sigh. "Hold on." He walked, not in any particular hurry, mind you, to get the hose. When he returned, he opened the nozzle.

My whole front got soaked. "Hey!"

"Sorry." He smirked. He *wasn't* sorry. After adjusting the water volume, Drew sprayed off my foot until I couldn't see any more of the vile, putrid substance.

I lowered my foot, carefully avoiding that pile or any other and dried off on the grass. "Thanks for the *shower.*" I glanced down and then back up. Drew's gaze was stuck on a particular part of me. *Ugh.* If I'd intended on being in a wet tee-shirt contest, I'd at least hope for a prize if I won. *No freebies, mister.* I crossed my arms over my soggy shirt.

"Sorry. Really." Drew reached out his hand. "Here, let's go rescue my *dog* from your *cat.*"

"My...hey wait a minute."

Drew laughed.

Right. How could I have forgotten the way he used to tease people? Not so much me, because he didn't really talk to me all that much, but everyone else. I thought he'd let go of my hand once I was vertical, but he didn't. How many times over the years had I dreamed of him doing just that, but he never had? I'd imagine him lacing his fingers through mine, then letting go to wrap his arms around me. He'd lean close and his lips would—

"—Okay?"

Huh?

"You zoned out there for a minute."

"Sorry."

He tugged me to our pets and only then released my hand. Suddenly, even in the intense summer heat, my skin was cold. And lonely. Drew bent down to grab Chubbs, but my cat wasn't being very cooperative.

Chubbs hissed and swatted at Drew's hand.

"Hey!" Drew checked his fingers over, front and back. "What's up with your cat?"

"Maybe he's freaked 'cause he was chased by your dog."

Drew ran his hand over the back of his neck. What I wouldn't give to touch him there. And other places...

"Maybe you should..."

What? Startled, I could only stare at him. I gulped in a mouthful of air. Had I spoken the thought out loud? Did he really mean for me to—

Drew tilted his head toward Chubbs.

Oops. "Yeah." I crept forward and crouched down, glad to be on the patio so I'd hopefully avoid any more unpleasant introductions to the dog's byproduct. I made kissy noises.

"What are you doing?" Drew leaned close to me. His woodsy aftershave mixed with a scent that was definitely male—in a good way—nearly did me in.

I shrugged. "Chubbs is kind of...high strung. Making that noise is the only thing he'll respond to when he's scared." When I held out my hand, Chubbs darted toward me and leaped into my arms. After blowing some of his cat hair from my mouth, I stood up, holding him close. "My poor little Chubbsy."

If I hadn't looked right at that moment, I might have missed Drew rolling his eyes.

"What?" I said. "Don't you think of your dog, uh, whatever his name is, as your baby?"

He bit his lip. Trying not to tease me again? "His name is Blueprint. Hadn't really thought about it, I guess. Cora, how come I don't remember you being this softhearted in school?"

Maybe 'cause you hardly spoke to me? "I dunno."

Drew reached out to pet Chubbs but seemed to change his mind and pulled his hand back. "So, now that all the livestock is accounted for and unharmed, it's good to see you."

"You too." My gaze strayed toward the house, but I forced my attention back on Drew. "How are your parents?"

"They're good. They moved to California."

"So you..." I glanced toward the house again and back.

"Yeah. The house was my grandfather's. When he passed away, he left it to me in the event that my folks ever decided to move. When my dad accepted another job in California a few months ago, I took ownership."

"Oh." *So we're neighbors. Again.*

Drew smiled. "And you?"

"Me?"

"I haven't seen your parents around since I moved in. They all right?"

"Yep. My dad has a temporary job in Florida for a year. So Chubbs and I are house-sitting. Since college graduation last month, I was kind of floating around anyway. Needed a place to land."

"Ah." Was he running out of things to say?

"I assume you just graduated too?"

He nodded.

"And…" I wound one hand in a circle while still holding Chubbs with the other.

"And…I *didn't* flunk out." One corner of his mouth rose.

I laughed. "That's good to know. Wouldn't want to live next door to a dunce. But you knew I meant…what do you *do?*"

"I'm an engineer. Just got on at Community Builders, but I won't start there for a couple more weeks."

Boring…"How interesting."

"I'm hoping I'm not living next to a dunce, either, Cora."

"Rest assured I passed."

"And you are…"

Infatuated with you.

He raised his eyebrows and waited.

Oh, I'm supposed to say something. "I'm a romance novelist."

He blinked. Twice. "Ah."

What did *ah* mean? He sounded decidedly unimpressed. "Maybe I should go—"

"I was hoping we could catch up. Wanna stay for a glass of wine?"

At that moment, I didn't give a rat's patootie if Drew was impressed with my vocation or not. Drew Dunkirk had just asked me on a date!

Sort of…

Take what you can get, Cora.

CHAPTER TWO
Drew

I WENT INSIDE to grab some glasses and a bottle of red wine. Truth be told, I'd already had a glass and a half, needing something to calm my nerves. Cora had wanted to take her cat back to her house and retrieve her suitcase from the front porch where she'd dropped it. And she said she left the front door open. *Open.* Who does that? Wasn't she worried about some nut just walking into her parents' house and stealing everything in sight?

But man, Cora looked great. I didn't remember her being so curvy before. Apparently college life had been good to her. *Something* had been. I could barely keep my eyes off her. Especially when I accidentally got her shirt all wet and then her—

Stop now, Drew, before you get yourself into trouble. Tonight was just two old classmates getting together for a drink. It wouldn't go any further than that, right?

Right?

That was my intention, but...Cora was so attractive. I'd always thought she was cute. I'd sure had enough opportunities to be near her since our last names always put us side by side in homeroom class every year of high school. But dating Wendy Wilkinson the whole way through high school kept most of my focus off anyone else. Big mistake there. Once I got some time away at college and away from *her*, I realized how clingy and possessive she'd been. Having the opportunity to meet other girls showed me that they weren't all like that.

Besides, it might not have worked with Cora anyway. I was captain of the chess club, for Pete's sake, and she was...

Cora came across as free as the breeze, drifting to whatever caught her interest at any moment. Surely I would have been boring to her. Too safe. Stale. She had gravitated toward kids who were artists and in the drama club. And were writers on the school newspaper.

A romance writer...Did they have more interest in the opposite sex? Strictly for educational purposes, of course. I sure wouldn't mind being her test subject if—

A knock came from my back door.

"Be right there." I opened the door. Cora had changed into a pale yellow sundress and white sandals. Her long dark hair was up in a ponytail, the curly ends brushing against her neck.

"Sorry it took so long. I had to take a quick shower." She squinted. "Well, *another* shower." Her full lips curved up.

I grabbed the glasses and wine from the kitchen table and stepped outside next to her. "Sorry about that. Really."

"You're off the hook."

"I am?"

"Lucky for you it's a hot day, so the icy water didn't feel awful. Now if it had been January..."

"Then I'm guessing you might *not* have been barefooted."

Cora shook her head, causing her ponytail to bounce. "You never know, Mr. Dunkirk. A girl has to keep a few secrets. How do you know I *ever* wear shoes? Maybe I'm a member of some bizarre footwear-optional club."

I set the glasses and bottle on the patio table and then pointed down. "You're wearing shoes now. Must not be much of a secret."

She lowered her voice. "Please don't tell the other club members. I had to wear shoes today for self-preservation."

"Why's that?"

Her grimace was almost as cute as her smile. "If I encountered another unpleasant, er, deposit, I'd rather have something between it and my *bare* skin."

Bare skin...Feet, shoulders, legs, neck..."Right." I filled both wine glasses and slid one in front of her. "So, tell me about your writing."

"You really want to know?"

"Sure."

"Before you hadn't seemed..." She eyed her wine.

"What?"

"I wasn't sure you were interested."

"I'm definitely interested. In you. Uh, in what you do...I mean, in your work." I gulped a hefty drink of my wine before I spewed any more stupid crap. *Idiot.*

She pursed her lips and then took several sips from her glass. Was she trying not to smile? "Okay, well, I was an English Lit major in college. I could have gone into teaching, and still might if writing doesn't pan out. But honestly, I just adore writing. Creating new worlds. Inventing characters. Telling them what to say and how to feel and act. It's such a wonderful way of expressing my feelings."

"I can't imagine having that kind of talent."

Her cheeks flushed pink. "Oh, um, thanks."

"Maybe you'll let me read some of your writing some time?"

Cora nearly choked on her wine. "Y-you'd want to—"

"Sure." Was she kidding? Anything to get to know her better.

"I'm not sure that's such a good—"

I leaned forward and rubbed the back of her hand. "Ah, c'mon. Not even for your former neighbor?" The wine must have taken affect. I wasn't usually quick to touch someone I didn't know well. But I felt like I did know her after all those years of sitting side by side in school and living next door.

"Not former. Neighbor. *Again.*"

"True." Why did it freak her out so much that I

wanted to read her books? "Hey, I forgot the crackers and cheese." I stood. "Be right back."

I had forgotten them, but what I really wanted to get was a second bottle of wine. I liked how drinking it had made me feel braver around her. Loosened my tongue. Maybe if I drank more, I could tell her that I'd always admired her, always thought she was pretty and interesting.

I hurried inside and grabbed the food and another bottle. With my arms full, I hipped the screen door open and let it slam shut after I was back outside.

"Oh! Let me help you." Cora stood and hurried over.

She reached up and snagged the wine from the crook of my arm, her fingers brushing my skin. A tingle danced across my arm. "Thanks." I set the food on the table.

Cora eyed the bottle. "You must *really* like wine. We haven't even finished the first one."

Did she think I had a drinking problem? Truth was, I didn't usually drink very much. I shrugged, hoping it came off as nonchalant. "It's a special occasion."

"It is?"

"Sure it's...Neighbor Re-acquaintance Day."

With a sputtered laugh, she reclaimed her chair. I sat down too, wishing my chair was scooted closer to hers, or that I dared to move it.

"Drew, you always could cheer me up."

Why had I not known that? "Really?"

"You were always cracking those jokes in homeroom."

I told jokes to try to make Wendy laugh. That was obviously a waste of time. "Guess somebody had to lighten the somber mood at 8:30 every morning."

She sipped her wine. "True. Getting up that early was brutal. I've always been a night owl. Even then."

"Is that when romance authors find their muse?"

"Muse? Most non-writers don't use that word."

"I'm deep, Cora. *Very* deep."

She laughed again. In high school, she'd had an infectious giggle, but now maturity enhanced her voice. The effect was a slow, sexy sound that went straight through me to my toes.

My favorite rock music blared from my phone in the belt holder at my hip. I glared at the despicable piece of technology. Distraction was the last thing I needed or wanted at the moment.

Cora tilted her head. "Aren't you going to answer it? Might be important."

I retrieved the phone and checked the caller ID. "It's my mom. I'll call her later." The music went silent, but it had given me an idea. I stood. "Wait here."

"Where else would I go?"

"I dunno. Didn't want you to get any crazy ideas and start hanging from my fence again. Like a possum."

Her chuckle followed me to a small table that sat beneath the awning. The radio I kept there was pre-set to an easy-listening station, and I hit the button.

Cora smiled. "That's nice." She swayed in her seat to the tune, her eyes half closed.

I took a gulp of wine to bolster my confidence and held out my hand. *Now or never, Drew.* "Dance?"

Her eyes popped open. "You wanna dance? With *me?*"

"I don't think my dog can stand up long enough to be my partner, so yeah..."

She set down her glass and stood, darting a glance around at everything but me. Was she nervous? Because of me? Surely not. I stepped closer and gathered her in my arms before she could change her mind.

Cora fit very nicely in my arms. Better than I'd even imagined. Her hair smelled like lilacs and her shoulders of soap. "Mmm. You smell really nice."

She tensed. "Um...thanks."

Did I actually just say that? "I mean..."

She raised her chin from my shoulder. Her pretty brown eyes were surrounded by dark, long lashes. "That was sweet of you to say."

I nodded, lost in the depths of her eyes, my gaze then lowering to her lips, unable to focus on anything else. Was I dreaming? I was holding her, dancing with her. How could the moment get any better?

You should kiss her, you dork.

I couldn't kiss her yet. It was too soon. What would she think? Then again, I might not have a chance again, and I didn't want to blow it. It was now or never. I placed my hand beneath her chin. I hesitated and watched her for any sign that I might get slapped instead of kissed.

Cora stared steadily back at me, a small smile playing on her mouth. As I lowered my lips toward hers, she closed her eyes. She wanted it too.

The instant our lips met, a shock went through me. She tasted even better than I'd thought she might.

This might be the start of something big.

CHAPTER THREE
Cora

I PULLED ON my gardening gloves and grabbed my trowel. My side of Drew's fence was looking pretty shabby. Time to do away with some weeds. Kneeling down, I grabbed the top of a big cactus-like thistle and yanked. Those roots must have been deep, because I ended up on my backside.

Tossing the weed to the side, I got up and went after another. I frowned. Vile plants. They had no business taking up residence in my yard. I smiled, however, when I thought of Drew. I'd been surprised by the kiss but oh, so pleased. I still couldn't believe he had done it. *Drew...*

His kisses had melted my toes. And we'd danced and kissed and—

A sudden pain shot out over my right eye. Ah yes. The wine. Would Drew have kissed me if we hadn't been drinking?

Something soft brushed my leg, and I jumped. "Hey, Chubbs." I reached out my hand to pet him, but he recoiled from my glove.

"It's not a puppet, honey. Just a glove." Guess I

shouldn't have teased him with that dog puppet when I first got him. Chubbs hissed and hurried away toward the other end of the fence.

A scratching sound followed. Now what? I pivoted in the grass. My cat now sat on top of the fence. "Chubbs, that is not your personal observation tower." I stood and brushed dirt from my shorts.

Another scratching sound came from the fence. From the other side. Chubbs wasn't moving but his fur stood on end. *Not good.*

I hurried toward him, ready to grab him and stuff him back in the house. Before I could get my hands around him, a loud bark sent a shiver over my scalp, nearly scaring me hairless. I took a gasp of air and peered over the fence.

"Blueprint, honestly. Keep that up and Chubbs and I will both be bald."

Another bark, this one sounding like the canine form of a chuckle, had Chubbs leaping into the air. I leaned over the fence but Chubbs had attached himself to the tree on Drew's side.

Where was Drew, anyway? This would be a good time for him to show up and get his mangy mutt away from my cat. Maybe he was inside his house. "Drew? You home?"

No answer except doggy panting and cat hissing. Perfect.

Guess it was up to me. I held out my arms. "Here, Chubbs. Come on down." Chubbs stared at my gloves. "Um, sorry." I removed the offending articles and tossed them to the ground. I held up my bare hands. "There, see? All gone. Will you come down now?"

In answer, my cat climbed higher. I groaned. I hated when he did that. The last time was outside my apartment at college. He'd stayed up there overnight. I'd been so worried that I'd missed my first two classes the next morning trying to get him down. A call to the fire department had been necessary. I'd been equally embarrassed when Chubbs had scratched the nice fireman who had climbed the ladder and finally grabbed Chubbs by the tummy.

I really did not want a repeat of that. If I called someone now, Drew was sure to hear about it even if he wasn't home when it happened.

"Oh, Chubbs." I shook my head. "Mommy doesn't need this today."

He climbed higher and howled.

There was no other choice. It was up to me. With a sigh, I climbed onto the top of the fence, grabbing a low branch as I teetered back and forth on my toes. I held tight with my hands braced on the limb and placed my bare foot on the rough bark.

"Ouch. Thanks so much for this, Chubbs!" I glanced up. His huge green eyes stared at me like a demented owl from halfway up the tree. "Why don't you just come down and save us both a lot of discomfort and embarrassment?" He meowed. "Fine, maybe you won't be embarrassed, but I will."

Chubbs reached out one paw and placed it three inches below where he sat. Was he coming down?

"Good boy! Come to Mommy."

Instead, he backed away and slid farther up the tree.

"Of course you did." Still straddled between the fence and tree, I swung my other leg up.

Blueprint barked, startling me so I nearly dislodged my grip. I glared down at him. "Now cut that out."

The dog whined and sat on his haunches.

"Sorry, Blueprint. I know you're just being a dog. Can't help it, I suppose."

He stuck his tongue out the side of his mouth and panted. I squinted. Was he...smiling?

But when I returned my focus to Chubbs, he seemed anything but pleased. His tail lashed against the tree, his fur snagging on the bark.

"Okay, I'm coming." I hated shoes but this would have been a good time to have some. Man, that bark was *rough*. I pulled myself up to another limb, my toenail biting into the side of the tree.

"Chubbs, I'm not enjoying this, just so you know."

He whimpered and stared at me, unblinking.

"All right. I know you're not having fun either." I got another foothold and went up a few inches more. Making the mistake of peeking down, I gulped. I wasn't super high up, but anything more than a footstool made me dizzy.

After taking a deep breath and vowing not to look

down again, I climbed higher. Chubbs was still a few feet above me. "Couldn't you come to me? Then maybe I could carry you down the rest of the way." Although, I wasn't sure how that was going to work since I'd need both hands firmly wrapped around the tree so I wouldn't fall. Maybe I could stuff Chubbs down the front of my shirt?

A glance at his sharp claws made me rethink that one. How would I explain to an ER doc the reason I had bloody claw marks on my breasts? He might think I was into something weird and report me.

However I could manage it, though, I needed to rescue my cat. Only one way to achieve that. I kept climbing. I reached up and grasped higher, standing on my tiptoes until I could swing one leg up then the other to the nearest thick foothold. Now I was up way too high. But Chubbs was still a few feet away. And he wasn't budging.

Maybe I needed to rest for a few minutes and try to reason things out. This would be an excellent time for Drew's engineer logic instead of my writer's imagination. It wasn't like I could write myself out of the tree.

I chuckled. Wouldn't that be nice?

I turned and settled into a fork that was molded like it had been made for someone to do exactly that. I edged back, shuddering when something crawled across my neck. "Ack!" With a swat, I hit the offending interloper. When I checked my palm, I grimaced. Perfect. Brown bug guts were smeared across my skin. I didn't want to wipe them on my clothes because...that was just gross. The only other option was the tree. Revulsion swept through me as I thought of what all was on my hand. Bug intestines? Bug gallbladder? "Blech!" I swiped my hand down the bark, wincing when a sharp piece poked me.

That's just great. Now I was bleeding. A gash an inch long spewed red. Not good. I didn't even have a bandage. They really should equip trees with first aid kits for instances like that. I'm sure I wasn't the first person to climb into a tree to rescue a cat.

I pressed my palm against my shirt, hoping to stop the blood-letting. Good grief, that cut wasn't that big. Must be deep, though. *Don't dwell on it, Cora. Remember what happened when you had to dissect that frog in*

Biology class. Passed out flat on the floor and the tiny woman who was your teacher couldn't lift you. And then the poor school janitor had to help. Clean up on aisle frog-girl.

I inhaled deeply, willing calm into my body and mind. I glanced down at my shirt. I'd never get all the blood out. And it was one of my *favorite* shirts. Sunny yellow and white lacy trim around the neckline. Bother. It would have been better to just smear the bug guts there.

I recovered enough to analyze my situation. It wasn't good. How was I going to get down? Get Chubbs down? Would he and I perish in the tree, clutching each other and confessing our regrets for lives being cut way too short?

"Blueprint? You out here?"

I gasped. Drew was home. *This is great! No, it's not.* What would he say when he saw me stuck in his tree? I wanted to make a good impression on him. Stranded up there with my cat and a cut hand and enough blood on my shirt to look like I'd murdered someone wasn't the way to achieve that.

No, I needed to stay quiet and wait for him to leave. Surely I'd be able to figure out something after that. Maybe I could jump. I shuddered, thoughts of broken bones jarring my brain. Not good either. But I really didn't want him to know I was there.

"Blueprint?" His voice was louder now. The dog barked. "Hey, boy." Drew was right *below* the tree. "What's going on?"

Just don't move. Hold your breath. Maybe Drew won't—

"Cora? What on earth are you doing in my tree?"

Cover blown. The jig was up. I glanced down but kept a tight hold of the nearest branch with my un-bloodied hand. "Uh...isn't it a lovely day?"

He frowned. "I guess. But that doesn't answer my question."

"I was, well...The clouds they're so pretty and I wanted to...see them."

"Couldn't you do that from down here?"

"This is...closer. Yeah, I can see them better. From here."

Grass rustled as Drew stepped forward. "Is that why Chubbs is there with you? To watch the clouds?"

My face heated. "Well, he...There was this bird and he wanted to—"

"Cora." He tapped his tennis shoe on the ground. "You're stuck, aren't you?"

"Um...kinda."

"Would you like some help?"

Realizing I wasn't going to get a better offer, *any* other offer, I nodded. "If you're not busy at the moment."

He shook his head. "It wouldn't matter if I was busy. I'm not leaving you up there."

I swallowed. What an idiot I was. *He must think I'm the biggest loser airhead the world has ever known.* "Okay. Thanks."

"Don't move. I'll be right back."

Where was he going?

The scrape of metal came from a few yards away. Drew dragged a partially rusted ladder over and leaned it against the trunk. In a matter of seconds, he had scaled the ladder and was face to face with me. "Why didn't you just use a ladder?"

Yeah, that would have been a great idea. "I...Chubbs was on the fence, and then Blueprint barked and scared him, and I was scared for Chubbs so I got on the fence and climbed the tree, and Chubbs went higher so I did too and—"

"Cora. Take a breath."

I did.

"Now another."

I breathed in deeply.

"Better?"

I nodded.

Drew tilted his head back. "Chubbs is three feet above you."

"Yeah I know. I was trying to get to him."

"You're really high up already. I would say you're at least—"

"Don't *tell* me. If I know how high I am, I'll get dizzy and fall, and then you'd have to—"

"Just relax. Let's try to get you down."

"I can't leave Chubbs up here, Drew! See how

helpless he is?"

With a sigh, Drew closed his eyes briefly. "All right. Stay here. Don't move. And *don't* look down."

"Don't worry."

Drew climbed further up the ladder. I followed his path with my gaze. Drew reached out to Chubbs, slowly. "Okay, kitty, let's get you down from—"

Chubbs swatted at Drew, hissed, and proceeded to hop to the branch closer to me.

I gasped. "*Chubbs.* If I'd have known you could do that, then I wouldn't have—"

One glance at Drew's lowered eyebrows silenced me. I watched, aghast as Chubbs continued to jump to each successive lower branch until he hopped down to the fence. Then into my yard.

I bit my lip and met Drew's eyes. "Honestly, I didn't know he could—"

He held up his hand. "Never mind that. We need to get you down." He descended a few rungs until he was even with me. His eyes widened. "You're stomach is bleeding!"

"No, it's…" I held up my hand, palm out.

He grimaced. "That looks bad. Has the bleeding stopped?"

I shook my head.

"All right. Here." He reached down and whipped off his tee shirt.

Holy cow. The man had muscles on his muscles. I blinked and forced my gaze away from his chest. "I couldn't. It will ruin your shirt and—"

"Who cares? Wrap this around your hand."

I did, trying not to inhale deeply because a little whiff told me that his shirt smelled really *really* great with his aftershave.

"Now," he said. "Let's get you down, okay?"

I nodded, still embarrassed at my predicament but so relieved Drew was there. "Thanks."

One side of his mouth rose in a smile. "No problem."

He leaned back away from the ladder a little. "I'm going to need you to get on the ladder."

"But *you're* there. I can't—"

"Yes you can. Come on. I want to stay close to you

since you only have one hand to climb with." He kept hold of the rung with one hand and opened out his other arm offering me room to squeeze between him and the ladder.

I let out a breath. I wasn't going to get any other offers of help. Slowly, I crab-crawled with my feet and good hand to the top of the ladder and stepped onto the warm metal. My other foot found its mark, and I slid down.

Now I was face to face with Drew, his arm around me. Heat from the rest of my body alerted me to the fact that his arm wasn't the only thing touching me. Chest. Legs...Oh boy.

I stared up at him, suddenly unable to breath.

Drew raised his eyebrows. "As nice as this is, you need to turn around so you can climb down the ladder."

"Right." My face heated as I turned, trying not to think which of his body parts was now pressed closely against my backside. I clutched the rung and began my descent. When I got to the fence, I carefully hopped to the ground. Within a few seconds, Drew was beside me.

What would he say? My desire to make a good impression on the man was now ruined. "I feel like an idiot. Thank you so much for saving me. And for—"

His finger on my lips stopped my words. "It's all right." He took me by my good hand and led me to my house.

Chubbs sat on the steps, lashing his tail and staring at the door like he'd been there all morning. I opened the door and glared at him. "This is all your fault."

My cat gazed up at me with huge, round eyes, suddenly all kittenish and innocent. He mewed.

My heart melted like it always did. Like Chubbs knew it would. "Kitty, I know you didn't do it on purpose."

Drew cleared his throat and sighed. "Come on. Let's get you inside."

At the kitchen sink, he ran warm water over my hand.

"Ow!" I tried to pull back, but Drew held firm.

"No. We need to clean it out so it doesn't get infected." He lathered soap on his hands and gently, as if he were stroking a butterfly's wings, worked the soap over my wound. He held it under the water and rinsed my hand, then his. Grabbing a paper towel from the nearly roll, Drew pressed it to my palm. "Go sit down at the table. I'll be right back."

I sat down. "Where are you going?"

"To get some supplies for your hand."

I heard him step into the bathroom. The door of the medicine cabinet squeaked open and then closed. My goodness he was resourceful when not even in his own house.

He reappeared. "All right. Now let's get you fixed up."

I nodded but didn't peer down at my hand as he bandaged me up. Instead I watched his face. His dark eyes squinted, brow furrowed in concentration, and eyelashes bumped his cheek when he blinked.

I sighed. Such perfection.

Drew glanced up. "You okay?"

I straightened in my chair. "Sure. Um, thanks. I appreciate this."

He shook his head and smiled. "I don't know what I'm going to do with you."

I had a few ideas.

CHAPTER FOUR
Drew

I RAN MY finger along Cora's arm. "Are you sure your hand is okay?"

"Yeah, it's fine." Cora's arm was at her side, the white bandage a startling contrast to her tanned skin.

"Maybe I should check it, just to be sure."

"I thought you were an engineer not a doctor."

I reached between us on the hammock and gently peeked beneath the bandage. Looked fine. No redness or swelling. "Just want to make sure I did an adequate job of taking care of you."

As Cora snuggled her shoulder into mine, the hammock rocked. "I've got to get one of these for my yard. This is fabulous."

"If you got one, would it come with an open invitation?"

A smile played on her lips. "For Chubbs? Sure."

"I meant for *me*."

"Oh...I guess."

I tickled her ribs until she shrieked. "You *guess?*"

"Ah! Stop...t-tickling me and I-I'll—"

"You'll what?"

"You can lie in my hammock."

I stopped the torture and ran my finger from her chin to the neckline of her shirt, loving the feel of her satiny soft skin. "But that's only part of the deal. I think you're leaving something out, Cora."

"What else is there? I get a hammock. You can lie in it."

"I wouldn't want to be there alone. Might be scary by myself. Monsters and all that."

"I already said Chubbs could use it too. He'd protect you."

"You know I wasn't talking about Chubbs."

"Oh, all right."

"Great."

"Blueprint can use it too."

"Cora..." I narrowed my eyes.

"What?" She was all innocence in appearance, but there was a gleam in her brown eyes.

"You knew I meant you and me."

She giggled. "Well, yeah."

I patted the side of the hammock. "Too bad I didn't have this when we were in high school."

"Why?"

"Maybe we could have...used it then like we are now."

"Even though we played together some when we were little, you didn't talk to me much in high school, so I doubt anything in a hammock would have occurred. Plus, Wendy always seemed to be glued to your side."

"That doesn't mean I didn't notice you."

"Ah." A pink blush colored her cheeks. "In any case, I'm sure your mom would have been *thrilled* for you to lie around in hammocks with girls when you were sixteen."

"True. Would've been fun though. Every teenage boy's dream."

Cora harrumphed. "And just *who* would have been invited to your hammock party?"

"I'm not at liberty to say. Highly confidential." I darted a sideways glance to her. "Who would have been at *yours?*"

"Mine's a secret too."

"And here I thought you were a tell-all romance

writer. This is certainly a disappointment."

"You've never read my books, so how would you even know?"

"I offered to read them earlier, remember?"

She lifted one shoulder in a shrug. "We'll see."

"What's that about? Aren't they available to the public? Couldn't I just go to the bookstore and buy one for myself?"

"Not yet. They're in editing with my publisher."

"But you have your own rough draft copy, right?"

"Maybe."

"Come on, Cora. I wanna read them." I tickled her face with a lock of her hair.

"Maybe when...I get to know you better."

"You're sharing my hammock. I'd say we've been introduced."

She laughed. "A girl needs to have a few secrets."

"Thought yours was not wearing shoes." I pointed to her bare feet.

"I'm allowed more than one secret."

I sighed. "This is getting me nowhere."

"Got that right. Hey, is there any of that soda left?" Cora tried to peek over her shoulder but nearly tumbled off the hammock in the process.

I grabbed her shoulders. "Easy there." I rolled over, nearly on top of her to grab the bottle from the grass.

From beneath me came a muffled. "Can't breathe..."

"Sorry." I leaned back, giving her some air. "Do you want the bottle, or should I serve you, my queen?"

"I like that—queen. Yes, slave. Serve me."

I uncapped the bottle and slipped my hand beneath her head so she could get her lips around the bottle. She took a few sips and then nodded that she was done.

Right before I recapped the bottle, I let a few drops fall onto her chest.

"Ah! What are you doing?"

"Hmmm. Gee, not sure how that could have happened."

"Right." Cora narrowed her eyes. "I'm coming to realize that your engineer brain does nothing without a plan behind your actions."

"Is that so? And just what reason might I have had

for that?" I pointed to one of the drops that was quickly rolling south, scurrying beneath Cora's shirt.

"Oh, that's cold!"

She started to sit up but I shook my head.

"What? I need to clean it off."

I grinned. "I can help."

"I don't need help grabbing a napkin from the kitchen."

"That's not part of the plan."

She lay back on the hammock and raised one eyebrow. "It's always *the plan*."

"Of course."

"So, are you going to tell me what it is before it dries on my skin and gets all sticky? I'd rather not attract bees. Bees are not my friends."

I watched as her lips formed into a pout. "If you really want to know."

"Just get it off, please."

"As you wish, your majesty." I leaned down and kissed her jaw, then her neck.

"What are you doing? I think you're forgetting the drops of soda."

"All in good time." I reached the first dark drop on her collarbone and ran my tongue across it. "Mmm, that must have been a very good year."

Cora jumped when I touched her. "The soda has a year?"

"No. You."

"Oh." Her throat moved when she swallowed.

I found the next drop, halfway between her collarbone and the top of her shirt. I licked the spot way more times than was necessary but what could I say? I was thorough.

She shivered and then glanced down at me. "Did you...get it all?"

I shook my head and raised one corner of my mouth.

With narrowed eyes, she said, "I know that expression."

"What expression?"

"You, my good man, are up to something."

"Ya think?"

"I *know*."

I plucked the fabric of her neckline and raised it from

her skin a couple of inches.

"Hey! What are you—"

"Patience..."

Cora shuddered when I ran my tongue down below her shirt, right above her bra.

She let out a breath. "Was there really soda down there?"

"I guess we'll never know."

"But *you* know."

"True." I laughed.

"You're wicked."

"You say that like it's a bad thing."

She giggled. "Get back up here."

I scooted up beside her. "Yes? How can I be of service?"

Cora wrapped her arms around me and pressed her lips to mine. I rubbed my hands up and down her back, my fingers lingering on her shoulder where there was bare skin. I kissed her there too, taking in her scent, now familiar.

I tangled one hand in her hair and rested my other on her back. Cora nudged my chin up with the top of her head and nestled against my neck.

She shifted slightly. "Hey, Drew?"

"Yeah?"

"Is your...uh, are you touching my butt?"

"No. But I can if you really want me to." I wiggled my eyebrows up and down.

"Not that I would mind or anything, but, you have one hand on my hair, and another on my back."

"That sounds about right."

"So...who's touching my—"

I reached down behind her and got a handful of fur. "Your cat accepted your invitation to visit a hammock. I guess he didn't hear the part about the hammock being at your house."

Cora rose up and looked to her right. "Honestly, Chubbs."

The cat edged closer to Cora's backside and purred. Loudly.

"This is certainly...romantic."

Cora got the giggles.

"What?"

"Chubbs is used to sleeping with me at night. Maybe he thought since I was lying down somewhere, it must mean he can go to sleep too."

I sighed. "As long as Blueprint doesn't decide to—"

My dog picked that moment to howl. *Wonderful.* A huge furry paw slapped Cora on the backside, just missing the cat by mere inches.

"Drew? Really!"

"It wasn't me. Honest." I held up my hands to show her.

"Chubbs hands aren't nearly big enough to—"

"Hands?"

"Paws, whatever."

Blueprint flopped his other paw on Cora. She peered over her shoulder. "Hello." She turned back to me. "You don't suppose he would try to—"

My seventy pound dog leaped into the air and landed square on top of all three of us. Chubbs hissed and jumped down, and I wrapped my arms around Cora to try to protect her.

"What is your dog *doing*?"

I glared at Blueprint. "Get down. Now."

He whined.

"Blueprint. I mean it."

He snuffled Cora's hair with his nose, which produced more giggles from her.

"Blueprint! Daddy is telling you to—"

"Daddy?" She snorted. "And you make fun of how I talk to Chubbs?"

I gritted my teeth together. I hadn't meant to say that in front of her. Sure didn't make for a very manly appearance, did it? I reached up and tried to push Blueprint's face from Cora, but my dog wasn't cooperating.

"Drew? What is that warm, wet…something is *running* down my neck."

"Oh no."

"What? What is it?" She grimaced.

"Blueprint is, uh, drooling."

"Ugh!" She tried to sit up but the dog pressed both of us down.

I attempted to shove him off of the hammock but he held his ground and lay down flat on top of us. "Blueprint!"

A groan and creak came from above our heads.

Not good.

I wrapped my arms around Cora's middle. "Hold on to me tight."

"Why?"

"Cause we're going down!"

The ropes holding the hammock quivered, lengthening as they unraveled bit by bit. And then—

We thudded onto the ground. Blueprint didn't budge. He peered at me over Cora's head with his brown soulful eyes and whimpered.

A muffled, "Drew?" came from beside me.

I glanced at her. "You okay?"

"Can you call your dog off now? He's kinda flattening me out like a pancake."

"Like I said. So romantic."

CHAPTER FIVE
Cora

I WOKE THE next morning knowing something wasn't right. After rubbing sleep from my eyes, I reached out for the familiar feel of Chubbs' soft fur on the pillow next to mine. All I felt was air.

I sat up fast. *That* was it. I hadn't been able to find my cat the evening before, so he'd spent the night outside. I hated that. *Hated* the thought of what might happen to him out there all alone. In the dark.

Though, of course I knew that cats probably weren't afraid of the dark, *I* was afraid. That was enough to send me into a panic.

I flipped the covers back and hopped from bed, getting a brief glance in the mirror as I hurried by. Medusa hair, wrinkled pajama bottoms, and an old white tee-shirt with a small hole in the left shoulder.

I normally wouldn't have wandered outside the confines of the house looking so frightful, but I had to make sure Chubbs was all right. After stepping out onto the porch, I scanned the area. No cat. Wasn't his tummy growling? Surely he'd be demanding breakfast soon.

To my left, a door squeaked open and then closed. Drew stood on his patio, patting Blueprint on the head. I glanced down at my wrinkled clothes and could only imagine what he'd think my pillow hair looked like. Maybe if I was quiet and left now, he wouldn't—

"Cora?"

Perfect. Now in the light of day, Drew would see how I really look without the benefits of a shower and blow-dryer. "Hey." I gave a wave and headed toward him.

He smiled, his white teeth gleaming in the sun. Part of his hair was damp. Had he just showered? I lowered my chin an inch and gave myself a discreet sniff. Not good.

"So..." He came to the fence and leaned his forearms on the top. "I really enjoyed last night."

I stepped back, not wanting to kill him with my morning-after-wine breath. "Yeah, me too."

"I was thinking maybe we could do something again tonight?"

My heart thumped out a hard beat worthy of any great rock drummer. Even with me resembling road-kill, he wanted to see me again? And unless he'd been drinking very early today, he wasn't under the influence of wine. "I'd like that." I glanced down. "Of course, I'd need to shower. And wash my hair, change clothes."

He tilted his head. "I think you look great."

"Maybe you need to visit your optometrist."

"Nah. I've always thought you..."

What's this? I stood up straighter. "I...what?"

Drew lifted one muscled shoulder in a shrug. "I've always thought you were..." His gaze drifted to somewhere over my left ear.

Don't stop now! I reached out and lightly touched his arm, still propped on the fence. "What?"

"It's nothing."

There was no way I was going to lose out on whatever it was he *wasn't* saying. "It must be something or you wouldn't have brought it up."

"All those years we sat next to each in school...I'd always thought..."

Gah. Mr. Engineer couldn't string a whole sentence together. Was it possible he'd noticed me like I'd noticed him? "Drew?"

"I used to think you were really cute."

My mouth went dry, and I swallowed. "You did?"

"Yeah." Something rustled in the grass. Was he shuffling his feet?

"Too bad you were dating Wendy every minute of high school."

He nodded. "Lesson learned on that one. So if it hadn't been for her, if I'd been unattached and had asked you out, what do you think you might have said?"

I don't think, I know. "I might have said yes."

Drew blinked. "Guess I blew it. Wasted all my time on the wrong girl."

Though nothing had been mentioned about him still being involved with Wendy, I'd assumed, well hoped, she was no longer in the picture. There had been those kisses, after all. And the hammock. "It's not too late." I smiled.

"Good to know." A light blush colored his cheeks. He glanced away, as if suddenly shy.

Something brushed against my leg, and I peered down. "Chubbs!" I scooped him up and pressed my face into his fur.

"Are you always so excited to see your cat? Didn't he just come outside with you?"

"No. He got locked out last night."

"Was he in trouble? Receive kitty time-out?"

"Of course not." I rubbed my hand over his back. "He'd never do anything to get in trouble."

Drew raised one eyebrow.

"Okay, not in *that* much trouble. I couldn't find him last night when I went to bed, so he had to stay out. My guess is he was close to the back door, sitting in the shadows, just outside of the reach of the porch light."

"Hmmm. I can certainly see why you think your little fur ball can do no wrong." He smirked.

"Very funny."

Chubbs squirmed until I set him on the grass. He trotted a few feet down the side of the fence and stood on his hind legs. What was he doing? I opened my eyes wide in shock. Chubbs had his front legs extended up, paws against the fence. Using it as a...*scratching post.* Though I hadn't meant to, I let out a gasp.

"What's wrong? Get bit by a mosquito?"

I whipped my gaze back to Drew. "No. It's nothing."

"You gasped. And stared down to your right. I thought maybe—hey, what's that sound? Like a scraping?"

I took a step to the side, toward Chubbs, hoping it was slow enough that Drew wouldn't notice. "I'm sure it's..."

"What?"

I slid to the right a little more. "It could be...uh..."

Drew leaned a little forward. Was he going to try to peek over the fence?

Another step and I was still three feet from Chubbs. "Maybe you have..."

"Have...what? Gnomes with tiny shovels?" He laughed.

"I was going to say...gophers." I held in another gasp when I saw what my cat had done. Eight gauges marred the wood of the fence, each divot several inches long. How many times had Chubbs done it? Surely that hadn't been the work of just that morning. Maybe he'd worked on it last night in a fit of rage, when he'd been locked out of the house. The cat did have a temper, after all.

Drew raised his eyebrows. "I don't think I have gophers. It's never been a problem before. Besides, if *I* have them—" He pointed down. "—then so do *you* since our yards are connected. Any anyway, the noise is coming from your side of the fence."

"Well, if not gophers, maybe...moles? Yeah moles. I bet that's it." The cat merrily continued his destruction of the fence, seeming not to care who saw or heard him.

"What is it? Maybe I should come over on your side and—"

Desperate to grab Chubbs and make him stop, I dove to the ground, tackling my cat. Chubbs howled but didn't claw me. I'd wrapped my fingers around his front paws and tucked his back feet under my arm. If I held on tight, maybe I could get him into the house before he went crazy.

"Cora?"

"I'm fine. We're fine. Everyone's..." I was on my knees then and leaned against the side of the fence. "Come on,

Chubbs," I whispered. "Work with me, here." Still clenching my squirming cat, I was finally able to slide up the side of the wood and stand. But not without at least two splinters embedded in the side of my arm.

Drew peered over the fence at me, eyebrows low over his eyes, arms crossed. "What in the world are you doing?"

"Just taking Chubbs in the house. It's his breakfast time and...I'd hate to see him become malnourished." As I rushed toward my back door, Drew's laughter followed me. I called over my shoulder. "Gotta shower and change. See ya later!"

If he didn't think I was crazy before, he will now.

As soon as we were inside, I shut the door and peeked out the kitchen door window. Drew stood at the fence, shaking his head. After a minute or so, he shrugged and walked back to his house. As fast as I could, I ran upstairs to shower and change. Then I went downstairs and through the kitchen to the attached garage.

I needed something to buff out those scratches. If I did a good enough job, would Drew even know it had ever happened?

Even though I'd never sanded anything in my entire life, it couldn't be that difficult, right? Dad used to sand down rough spots on wood he found around the house. It hadn't looked too daunting a task.

I spotted the sander next to several sheets of sand paper. Wait. I couldn't use a tool that would make noise. It had to be done as quietly as possibly so Drew wouldn't suspect anything. Instead, I picked up the sheets of paper and laid them side by side on the workbench. They all had different numbers. Did that have anything to do with how well they worked?

Needing all the help I could get, I chose the one that felt the roughest when I ran my thumb over it. Those gouges on the fence were deep. Better to get something that would smooth them out. The quicker the better.

With my sandpaper held close to my side to hide it, I sat on my back porch, wanting to make sure Drew wasn't outside. I didn't see him. A few seconds later, I heard his garage door raise and then lower. The engine of Drew's vehicle revved as it backed down his drive. Perfect. I could do the job, and Drew wouldn't even be around. I thought about running in to retrieve the sander, but what if he came back when I was using it? I might not be able to hear him over the motor.

I sat there a few more seconds to be sure he was gone. A thumping came from behind me. With a sigh, I rose and let Chubbs out again. If I didn't, he'd only get more insistent and scratch the inside of my door. After making sure he was all the way through the doorway, I closed the screen and hurried over to the site of the fence-mauling.

"*Chubbs.* Look what you've done." I knelt down in the grass, glad I'd thought to wear long pants. Didn't need any more chiggers leaving their unpleasant reminders on my legs.

As if he thought I'd wanted to really have a conversation with him, my cat trotted over from a few feet away. He rubbed against me and then the fence, as if they were the best of friends.

With a sigh, I bent down and started to rub the paper back and forth. Over and over. It was hard work. Realizing it was too much to try to go across all the scratches at once, I concentrated on only one at a time. I desperately hoped Drew would stay away well past the time it took me to do the job.

"Ouch!" If I got any more splinters in my hands, my skin would be raw. Too bad I'd ditched the only pair of work gloves I had after I'd found a spider had taken up residence, making a series of webs in the fingers of one glove. I shuddered. Nope. After that, I couldn't see putting it on my bare hand.

My knees were aching from kneeling so long. I sat down and crossed my legs, stretching forward and up a little farther to reach the scratched wood.

Something rustled the grass next to my left leg. I turned. Chubbs was rolling on his back, looking like a feisty kitten in the throes of a catnip overload. "Why did you have to cause destruction here, of all places? The fence doesn't even belong to us."

Chubbs purred and blinked his green eyes slowly closed then open. I rubbed the soft fur between his ears and sighed. "Only a mother could still want to pet you after the mayhem you've caused."

Better get back to it. I surveyed my progress. Three scratches looked much, much better. Actually, the wood surrounding them was smoother than the rest of the boards they were on. Would Drew notice? At least Chubbs hadn't done it on his side of the fence.

Or had he? Better check that out later, though I was fairly sure Drew would have said something had he noticed large, deep gashes in his fence,

With renewed vigor, hoping to finish before Drew returned, I scrubbed with the sand paper like a sailor would to a dirty ship's deck. So what if I chipped my fingernails and nearly bled to death from splinters and cuts? I *had* to get rid of the evidence of my cat's crime.

Finally, after smoothing the last scratch, I sat back and viewed my work. Not bad. The wood looked smooth and shiny, not rough like the rest of the wood, but wouldn't it be less noticeable than eight long scratches?

Pleased with the results, I stood, dusted the grass from the back of my pants, and headed toward the house.

Chubbs trotted after me and raced inside when I opened the back door. I stepped in and glared down at him. "See what you made Mommy do?" I held out my hands. "Now my manicure is all mangled."

He got on his hind legs and rubbed his face against my knee. I smiled, couldn't help it. Chubbs was so darn cute. "Yes, I love you too."

CHAPTER SIX
Cora

A KNOCK ON my back door diverted my attention from writing. And at a very critical paragraph too. Drew—I mean, my hero, was just leaning in for the first kiss with me—er, the heroine.

Hoping I didn't look too scraggly in my old jeans and pink tank top, I smoothed down my hair as best as I could on my way to the door. Through the window, I saw Drew. Anymore, when someone was at the back door, it was usually him. Which was all right with me. Quite all right.

As I opened the door, my smile fell. Drew's expression looked like that of a camper who only gets one week off from work a year and spent that week in the middle of a torrential rainstorm in a leaky tent. "Hey, Drew, what—"

His face was red. He let out a loud huff of air and pointed over his shoulder. "What. Is. That?"

I peeked past him into the yard. Everything looked okay. Wait. Chubbs had been outside for the last hour. Had he been taunting Blueprint from the fence again? "I don't know what you mean. What's the matter?"

"The matter is, my fence. *Somehow* it has several boards that now have large concave areas where I know they were perfectly straight before. And it's only on *your* side."

I bit my lip. Maybe I'd gone a little overboard with my sanding? Had smoothed more than I'd needed to? But it had looked fine to me when I'd checked it before I'd left it yesterday. I swallowed hard and twisted my hands together in front of me. "There's a really...amusing story here."

He crossed his arms. "You don't say."

I smiled sweetly, hoping to diffuse his foul mood before it worsened. "You see, I noticed yesterday that there were..."

"What?"

"There seemed to be...scratches?"

"Are you asking me or telling me?"

"Telling?"

"Cora, what in the world happened to my fence?"

I let out a sigh. "I'm sure he didn't do it on purpose. It's just what he does. What *they* do."

"He who?"

I glanced behind Drew right as Chubbs hopped onto the porch. The cat rubbed against Drew's leg as if they were best friends.

"Your cat made those concavities in the wood? How is that possible?"

"That's the funny part."

He raised one eyebrow.

"Okay, maybe not funny ha-ha."

"Instead of me standing here on your porch and you halfway out the door, why don't you come outside?"

Did I want that? To get closer to the scene of the crime, so to speak? Chubbs pawed at Drew's pant leg. Why was my cat being so friendly to Drew all of a sudden? Was he trying to apologize for scratching the fence?

I shook my head. That didn't sound like Chubbs at all. More likely he was gloating over the damage.

Drew tilted his head. "No..."

"No?"

"You were shaking your head."

I blinked. *Time to face the music.*

I opened the door a little wider, forcing Drew to take a single step back. I took my time in stepping onto the porch and closing the door. Anything to delay having to explain what happened. I turned and gave Drew my best smile. "Isn't it a beautiful day?"

He tapped his tennis shoe on the step. "It seems you know something about what happened. Care to fill me in?"

I chewed on my lower lip and nodded. "All right. Come on."

I trudged to the fence. Drew's footsteps swished through the grass right behind me. Something moved to my right. There was Chubbs, running toward the fence as if he hadn't seen it in decades.

To my horror, my cat went right back to the same exact spot in the fence and started scratching. Again. "Chubbs, no!"

"What the—" Drew hurried toward Chubbs.

I grabbed the cat before he could do any more damage, although, looking down on the fence from the top instead of straight on as I'd done the day before when I'd viewed it from the grass, I could indeed see concavities.

This is not good.

Drew stared at the spot where Chubbs had been scratching. He rubbed his hand down his face and took a deep breath. "All right. Let me take a wild guess here... Your cat scratched the fence and you..."

"I tried, I really tried, and I thought I'd fixed it."

"How?"

"Well..." I gestured lamely with my hand not wrapped around Chubbs. "When I saw the scratches, I wanted to repair the damage *before* you—" I snapped my mouth shut.

"Before I what? Saw what your asinine cat had done?"

"Hey, he's not—"

"So you decided you'd be sneaky and fix it before I knew what had happened."

"I really meant to—"

"I can't believe you were trying to get away with that. Seems a little underhanded to me."

I held up my one finger. "But—"

"What did you do? Sand it down within an inch of its life?"

I blinked. "Listen. I realize the damage was done to your property by my cat. But it isn't as if he did it on purpose."

Drew glared at Chubbs, who was...I stared at my cat. He looked like he was smirking. "You don't think so?" Drew pointed at Chubbs, who swatted at his hand. "Hey!"

I turned slightly to keep my cat and Drew apart. "You *did* put your finger in his face, after all. Don't you hate it when someone does that to you?"

Drew let out a long, slow breath. "Cora, we're getting off track here. We were talking about my fence."

Why was he so upset about an inanimate object? "I'll be glad to pay for the damages if you want to replace the ruined boards."

"That's not even the point. I thought we were starting something between us. Maybe even trusting each other."

"I'm sorry this happened. I really am. I did my best to fix it, but obviously, I didn't know what I was doing."

"Obviously."

"That was *rude*."

"What was rude was trying to cover up what your stupid cat did and sneak around to try to fix it. Why didn't you just say something to me? I could have repaired the damage so it didn't look like a rhinoceros had stepped on it and left huge dips in the wood."

"Now you're just being silly. I can't imagine a rhino would—"

He held up his hand. "*Stop. Talking.*"

Anger boiled up from somewhere deep inside. The nerve. Here I'd tried to do something to take care of the problem myself and not bother Drew about it. Attempted to make his fence look the way it had before, prior to my cat doing what cats naturally do. There wasn't call for Drew to throw out mean adjectives about Chubbs. "You can't tell me to stop talking."

"I just did."

"Well, too bad."

His face reddened slightly. "Okay, look. I shouldn't have said that."

"Which part?"

"About you not talking. I realize as a writer you might not be able to help it. Can't contain all the silly things floating around in your head." He flapped his hand in my direction.

I gasped. "How dare you?"

"What?"

I pointed at his face, knowing full well I was doing what I'd accused him of, moments before. I didn't care. "Disparage my profession."

"I wouldn't call it disparaging. More like—"

"Besides that, you insulted my best friend."

He frowned. "Your...who?"

"Chubbs."

He bit his lips and his nostrils flared. Was he trying not to laugh?

"You are the rudest man I've ever met. While I'm sorry that this happened to your fence, and I might be a *little* remorseful that I tried to fix it and not tell you, your reaction is over the top." I turned and stomped away, holding tight to Chubbs so he wouldn't jump down and head back to Drew.

Because that would totally ruin my irritated exit.

"Cora? Wait! Come back."

Without even peeking over my shoulder, I said, "Don't bother coming to see me again. Until you're ready to apologize. To me and to my cat."

I carried Chubbs inside, shut and locked the door, and closed the curtains. I didn't want to talk to Drew right then or even see him. Because if he turned those big dark eyes on me and gave me that adorable smile, I might just cave in and—

No. I was still too upset. I needed to cool down, needed time away from Drew. I'd never seen that side of him. Didn't know he even had much of a temper. Guess it was good to find out before things between us had progressed any further.

I shook my head. All that irritation over a fence. I'd offered to pay for the damages. Why couldn't he have accepted that so we could move on? Pick up where we'd left off?

Fences were only practical for dividing things. And people. What a jerk. What had I been thinking, pining away for him all those years? And I'd danced with him. Touched my lips to his. Accepted his caresses. I hadn't said no. I'd been a willing participant. *Very* willing.

But no more. Mr. Engineer could just shove his fence someplace painful. I'd be first in line to see that. How dare he disparage what I do for a living? Put down something he knows nothing about?

Out of steam from my tirade, I went into the living room and plopped down on the couch. Chubbs followed and wound against my legs and then sat on my bare feet.

"Chubbs, my feet aren't cold, so I don't need a warm-up. But thanks, anyway." I picked him up and pressed my face into his soft fur. "I'm so irritated right now."

Chubbs squirmed.

"No, not with you. With Drew. Remember how I told you that I'd always had a big crush on him? Well, I let him kiss me, more than once, but just now he yelled at me. Who does that? Switches from one mood to another? And to think I've based all of my romance novel heroes on *him*. When he asked to read my books. I was actually considering letting him. What if he had recognized himself in the heroes? What a disaster *that* would have been. Then he would have known I've had feelings for him for a long time now."

A loud purr erupted from beneath the fur.

"Aw, thanks, dude. I love you too. Maybe it's good Drew showed his true colors before we went any further."

But I had really, *really* hoped it could turn into more.

CHAPTER SEVEN
Drew

As I stood on my patio, I thought about what a jackass I'd been the day before. How could I have flown off the handle like that about a fence? Sure I put a lot of time and effort into it, but it wasn't Cora's fault if her crazy cat decided to use it as a personal scratching post.

I continued to water the red geraniums that my mom had planted last year. They were pretty, I guessed, though I doubt I would have thought to plant them. I bet Cora liked flowers. Maybe I could take her some. Smooth things over.

I needed to apologize, somehow. My stupid pride was still poking me, so a straight out *I'm sorry* might not cut it. Could I sort of ease my way into a conversation with her by saying something funny?

A screen door slammed at Cora's house. She walked down her back steps carrying a small laundry basket. I glanced around. There wasn't a clothesline. Where was she going to hang something up?

Cora came nearer to the fence. Did she want to talk

to me? I turned off the hose and set it down. Wiping my damp hands on my jeans, I made my way over to her. "Hey."

"Hey." Her gaze didn't quite meet mine.

"So...about yesterday. Guess I was kinda acting like a jackass."

"Kinda."

She wasn't smiling. At all. Time to try again. "Listen, I said some things and—"

"Yeah, you did say some things."

I rubbed my hand over the back of my neck. "I'm sorry about that."

"But not about how you overreacted?"

I shrugged. "I still firmly believe that I was right and—"

She held up her hand to stop me. "Whatever."

When she placed the laundry basket on the grass, I could make out several different colors of fabric. What was it? I leaned forward a little, but it still just looked like a small jumble of brightly colored clothes of some sort. I pointed. "What're you gonna do with those?"

She finally gave a smile, but it wasn't a friendly one. More like she was up to something and I was the one who would come out behind. "Hang them up to dry."

"There's no clothesline, so where..."

She fluttered her eyelashes at me, slowly.

Oh no. She wouldn't.

Cora reached down and plucked out something the color of a kiwi from the basket.

It was a bra.

"Wait, you can't possibly—"

"Do I look like I care? Is someone gonna haul me off to the fence pokey?"

She draped the green bra over a post so most of it was visible on my side of the fence. The shiny fabric sparkled in the bright sunlight. Then she leaned down and grabbed something else. Another bra. This one resembled a ripe grape.

"Cora."

When she retrieved something else, I held up my hand. "Is this really necessary?"

She plunked a strawberry-colored strapless thing

along with the others. "Necessary? Why, no."

"Then could you please—"

"Uh, no. I need to dry my lingerie and this is a perfect spot."

"Lingerie? With those colors it's more like a fruit salad."

"Like you would know anything about women's underwear."

How had this conversation gone from awful to terrible so fast? I managed a grin. "Of course I don't *know*. Can't remember the last time I wore one of those. Although, I'm sure they look much better on you." There. That should help.

She snorted. "You can rest assured that's something *you'll* never see. Sorry about your luck." She deposited a blueberry bra on the fence and then waved as she trounced away.

I watched her make her way across the yard and up her back steps. The way that woman wore those tight blue jeans should be a crime. I tugged at my shirt collar. Was the temperature rising? I know mine was.

Focus, Drew. Stop thinking about that and figure out how to make things up to Cora. My gaze floated to the fence. Kinda hard to stop thinking about *that* when she'd left her fancy bras right where I could see them.

Hmm. What would she think if I contributed to the collection? I hurried into the house and grabbed some clean underwear from my drawer. *Let's add something to her little art exhibit out there.*

When I reached the fence, I spotted Cora staring out her kitchen window. Good. That way I wouldn't have to point out what I was doing. With care, I unrolled each pair of underwear and placed them in between her bras. Now it was boy-girl-boy-girl.

It only took fifteen seconds. Cora came back outside and stomped over to me. "What do you think you're doing?"

"Hanging out my laundry."

"Somehow I don't think your tighty-whiteys should be in the mix."

"You don't like men's underwear?"

A full blush crept over her cheeks. "I...um."

I stepped closer. "Come on. I know you secretly want to wear them."

A one-sided grin appeared on her lips. But only for a second and it was gone. "No. I really don't."

Rats. Thought I'd made inroads there. "Listen, I really—"

Blueprint raced past me and rose on his hind legs against the fence. What was he doing? I glanced to where he was staring. Cora's silly cat sat perched on one of the fence posts. When had *he* gotten there?

"*Chubbs.*" Cora tried to grab her cat, but the wily thing evaded her grasp. In her bare feet as usual, Cora slipped on the grass. And didn't get up.

"Cora?" I scaled the fence and landed down beside her. "Are you hurt?"

Tears sat on the edges of her lower lashes. "My ankle..."

"Aww, let me see." I carefully lifted her lower leg and eyed her ankle. "Can you move it?"

She slowly wound it in a circle. "Yeah, but it hurts like crazy."

"I'm sorry. The good news is if you can move it, it's probably not broken." I scooped her up in my arms, stood, and headed for her house.

"*Hey.* What are you doing?"

"You can't very well walk up those steps by yourself, now can you?"

"Not exactly."

I smiled when she sighed and rested her head against my shoulder. The scent of lilacs drifted up to me. "Ah..."

"What's wrong?"

"Nothing. Just...nothing." When I'd maneuvered the steps, I tried to figure out how to open the screen door without releasing Cora. I could have set her down for a moment, but I didn't *want* to.

"Here. Let me." Cora leaned partway over and grabbed the door handle, giving me just enough room to wedge my foot in the opening and shoulder the door open the rest of the way.

The kitchen had been repainted yellow from its former white. Of course until recently, it had been years since I'd been there. Not that I was there very often since

Cora and I hadn't been best friends or anything. Mainly, I would make up excuses to stop by. See if her dad needed help paving the driveway. Or mowing the lawn.

Anything to catch another glimpse of Cora.

"Where to, madam?"

She snorted. "At least you didn't call me ma'am and make me feel old. How about the couch in the living room?"

I left the kitchen, passed through the dining room, and reached the couch. When I leaned down to place Cora there, her arms were still locked around my neck. I lost my balance and barely got my hand under me on the side of the couch before I would have fallen right on top of her.

Not that I would have complained.

"Oh!" Cora's eyes widened. "Are you—"

I stood. "Yeah. Fine." I needed some reason to stay longer. "Can I get you something cold to drink?"

Cora blinked, her long eyelashes bumping her cheeks. "Um, sure. That would be nice. Do you know where—"

I gave a backward wave. "Got it covered." A large pitcher of lemonade sat in the fridge. I poured two glasses and carried them back to the couch.

Cora reached out for the glass. "Thanks. That was very sweet of you." She sipped her drink.

I shrugged. "It was my dog who chased your cat, causing you to fall, after all." Without being invited, I sat on the edge of the couch. If it made her mad, she could always shove me off.

But I hoped she wouldn't.

Taking a big chance, I set my glass on the coffee table and then did the same with Cora's. She scrunched her eyebrows into a frown. I leaned forward and placed my hand behind her head. When I pressed my lips to hers, she didn't put up a fuss. I tilted my head, deepening the kiss. My blood was on fire, my heart crashing against my chest.

She reached up one hand and placed it on my chest. With the other, she touched my face, running small circles on my cheek with her warm fingertips.

Have mercy...

I wasn't sure where all that would lead, but I wasn't

going to argue. I was startled from my thoughts when Cora pulled away.

"This doesn't change anything about the fence, you know."

"I know." And I stole possession of her lips again.

CHAPTER EIGHT
Cora

I PRESSED MY fingers to my lips, remembering the feel of Drew's kiss. The warmth of his hands as they rubbed up and down my back. Had it really happened? I'd thought the first night's kiss was a fluke because of the wine, but now I wasn't so sure.

Still, I'd meant what I'd said about the fence. He'd totally overreacted. It was just a stupid bunch of boards nailed together. What gave him the right to unload on me about it? Time to grab the attention of the fence-loving engineer.

I grinned and went into the house. When I came back out, Drew wasn't in sight. Perfect.

With care, I spread out several pairs of my dainty underwear that matched in color the bras from the day before, on the top of the fence.

Let's see how you like that. I was determined to teach him a lesson for what he'd said about my vocation. And about the importance of what I do for a living. What I love. How I support myself. What was a fence but a pile of firewood-in-waiting? It was just a thing. My writing was art. A way of expressing myself and giving others a fun type of entertainment.

I skittered away and went back inside to email my latest round of revisions to my editor. I'd meant to do it the night before, but then that whole kissing thing happened. Priorities, ya know?

When I walked out the door again, Drew was cooking something on his grill. Whatever it was smelled divine. Right when I was going to try to finagle an invitation for lunch, loud voices erupted from the kitchen door, which was propped open.

Three men laughed as they walked outside, each carrying a beer.

Starting early, guys? If they were drinking now, what would they be like tonight? I sat down on the steps wanting to watch them but hoping not to be noticed. I felt like a spy, however, my curiosity got the better of me. In that department, I could give Chubbs some lessons.

I didn't recognize the other guys as being from high school. Maybe they were Drew's college friends.

I wondered what they would think about the underwear. I smiled. If asked, I could always say it was Drew's secret stash. Wouldn't he just love *that?*

Chubbs came from around the front of the house and sat at the bottom of the steps, staring at me with his huge green eyes. His tail twitched as if he was irritated that I would dare sit on the back steps where he liked to sleep.

I held out my hand and kept my voice low. "C'mere, Chubbsy."

He started up the steps but stopped on the second one from the bottom. What was he doing? Something caught his attention from Drew's yard. Was it the cooking smells?

I know what's coming next...

Chubbs sat back on his haunches and howled. Loudly. He always did that when he wanted fed. Normally I didn't mind because we would be inside. But now was not a good time.

I held out my hand trying to coax him to me. I didn't want to just reach down and grab him because then Drew might spot me spying on him.

Chubbs howled again.

Stop it!

Drew quit talking mid-sentence and turned in my direction. *Perfect.* He spotted me and waved. I tried to shrink back against the door even though it was obvious he knew I was there. He started toward my house, but halfway across his yard, he stopped, tilting his head as he stared at the fence. Pivoting, Drew went back to his friends. He said something to one of them and pointed to my underwear.

Uh-oh.

The other guy went into the house and came back with a big electric fan plugged into an extension cord. What in the world was he doing with a fan *outside?*

In fascination, I watched Drew position the fan right behind the grill. Was he trying to cool off the meat? Wasn't that counterproductive to the whole cooking with heat idea?

Chubbs stopped in mid-howl and stared at Drew's house. Then he ran full speed toward the fence. In one fluid movement, my fat cat landed on top.

Right next to my underwear.

Chubbs started howling again which brought loads of amusement, at my expense I was sure, from the guys. Especially Drew. He wiped his eyes with the back of his hand. Was that from the smoke being blown on him or because he found my howling cat now sitting on my purple underwear so amusing? The only thing worse would be if Chubbs decided to *wear* my underwear.

Crazy howling cat. I wouldn't have put it past him.

Drew abandoned his chef duties and neared the fence. He had a gleam in his eyes, like he was up to something. It was homeroom all over again, when he would find someone to harass and joke about. It hadn't ever been me, though. Until now.

He reached out his hand toward my...He wouldn't! Drew snagged my strawberry undies and held them to his face. *Gah!* What did he think he was doing? I stood and headed toward him. What was he—Drew was sniffing—*sniffing* my underwear.

"Drew! Stop that right now."

The three guys standing by the grill were doubled over with laughter.

Drew held the underwear out to me. "Here. Might want to re-wash these."

My mouth dropped open. "Those are *clean.* I just washed them."

He shook his head. "They don't smell so clean anymore."

"Yeah, because you have your grubby paws on them."

"No, it's not that."

"Spit it out, Drew. What are you talking about?"

"I'm not really sure how it happened, but *somehow* your panties have a faint—" He pulled them close to his nose again. "—no, *more* than a faint scent of...smoke." He raised one eyebrow and a slow grin spread across his mouth.

I gasped. "What? You mean you put the fan behind the grill so they would get smoky on purpose?"

"Why else would I have done it?"

"I thought because Chubbs was—" I snapped my lips shut.

"Having your cat howl was just a bonus."

"You are pure evil."

"You didn't think so last night, sweetums."

"Well last night I was...It wasn't...my ankle hurt!"

He glanced down. "Didn't seem to slow you down from barreling over here, did it?"

"It's, sort of, better today."

"So you won't need an amputation?"

"Of *course* not."

Drew shook his head sadly. "That's too bad."

"What?"

He pointed over his shoulder. "Jim over there in the red shirt—" Jim raised his beer. "—is a med student. I thought it might be good practice for him to have some useful surgical experience."

"Ugh!" I grabbed the underwear from Drew and then whisked the other pairs away too. "Come on, Chubbs. Let's go inside and away from these weirdoes."

I scowled at my cat when he totally ignored me and instead stared intently at the grill.

Traitor.

I turned and stomped to the house. Which I shouldn't have done, because when I reached the cement steps and continued the motion, renewed pain shot through my ankle.

I bit down on my lip, determined to get inside the house before Drew could see I was in pain again.

Amputation, my *foot*.

Duh, Cora, that was the idea...

I chuckled. I couldn't help it. Drew's comment about the med student and my ankle was funny. If it hadn't been at my expense, I would have laughed about it when he said it. Why was I so sensitive? Was it because of my writing? That I poured out my heart on the pages into my characters and didn't know how to shut off the emotions?

Or was it simply because Drew was the one who said it, and I didn't want to be the focus of his teasing. I did, however, want to be the focus of *other* things he did. A shiver went up my back.

I limped to the couch where I'd left my laptop. Might as well get some work done, since I was too embarrassed to go back outside. I was deep into my storyline when I glanced at the clock. Two hours had gone by.

Rubbing my eyes, I put aside the laptop and got up, testing my ankle. Not too bad. Resting it on the couch must have helped.

My stomach growled as I walked toward the kitchen, as if in anticipation of supper. My heart sank when I perused the fridge and cabinets. My parents hadn't left much food and I, of course, hadn't gone to the grocery yet.

Wonderful. I didn't feel like putting on some dreaded shoes and going out. I'd seen a jar of peanut butter in the cabinet. Ready to grab a spoon and just dig in, I stopped when someone knocked on my back door.

I hurried to the door and opened it. Drew stood there with a covered plate in one hand and my cat in the other. And Chubbs, squirming and growling, didn't look pleased.

"Hey, Cora." Drew stepped inside as if the underwear fiasco had never occurred. He placed Chubbs on the floor. Chubbs hissed and ran into the living room. "I caught your varmint up on the grill trying to help himself to a hamburger."

"Sounds like something he would do." I admitted to that but wasn't about to apologize to Drew after he'd made fun of me in front of his friends.

Drew shut the door and stepped closer to me. "Thought I'd bring a peace offering."

I really wanted to refuse, wanted to send him packing for being such a jerk. But when he lifted the napkin that covered the thick hamburger on a sesame seed bun, my stomach had other ideas. Still, I wasn't ready to let him off so easily. "Sure. It'll make a nice snack for Chubbs."

Drew lifted one eyebrow. "I brought it for you. If I'd wanted your cat to have some, I would have let him snatch one earlier."

My stomach growled. Loudly. Drew wouldn't believe me if I said I didn't want the food for myself. I shrugged, gave a one-side smile, then set the plate down on the table and went to the fridge for condiments.

"Wait. I already loaded it up for you."

I closed the fridge. "You did?"

He nodded. "Sweet pickles, ketchup, and mayo."

"That's my favorite way. How did you—"

Drew's gaze slipped from mine to the floor. He shrugged.

"No really. How did you know?"

"I might have noticed what you put on your burgers in the school cafeteria. Might have. Possibly."

How sweet. I stepped toward him and rose on my bare toes to place a light kiss on his cheek, which reddened. "Thank you."

"For the burger? You're welcome."

"That, yes, but...thank you for noticing how I liked it and for remembering it after all these years." I was so hungry but felt weird eating in front of Drew. "Would you like half? I'd be glad to split it with you."

He rubbed his stomach. "No thanks. Got a little carried away with the guys."

Ah. The guys. I couldn't stand it anymore. I had to eat. "Okay, you're welcome to come into the living room and watch me eat...that is, if you want."

One corner of his mouth rose. "Sounds like a plan. Need something to drink?"

"Sure," I said over my shoulder. "There should be some sodas in there. And grab one for yourself."

The fridge squeaked open and then closed. Drew came in bearing two cans of soda. I scooted over on the couch, making room for him. Drew tried to sit down next to me, but Chubbs had other plans.

My cat jumped up and settled against my leg, staring longingly at the food. With a sigh, I broke off a small piece of meat and held it out to him. He grabbed it in his mouth and trotted away.

Drew raised his eyebrows. "Where's he going?"

"Probably to my bed."

"He eats on your bed?"

"Sure. Where does Blueprint eat?"

"Well..."

"Come on." I waved my hamburger at him. "Confession time, Mr. Dunkirk."

"If you must know."

"I must."

He chuckled. "Blueprint eats his doggie treats..."

"Yes, go on."

"On my pillow."

I giggled. "At least Chubbs stays on top of my comforter." My smile fell. "At least I think he does. Hmm. Maybe I should start checking for kitty drool on my pillowcase before I go to sleep at night."

Drew eyed my hamburger. "Aren't you going to try it?"

I'd gotten so caught up in talking to him that I'd forgotten to eat. I'm not sure that had ever happened before. I took a big bite and swallowed. "It's heaven on a bun."

"I'm guessing that means you like it?"

I nodded, taking another bite. I closed my eyes. "Mmmm. That's as good as—" My eyes snapped open as my face heated. I couldn't say *that* to him.

"As good as...Come on, Cora. Don't keep me in suspense."

"Um as...chocolate. And I love chocolate."

"Uh huh. Sure..." He grinned and winked.

Oh, this is not good. Now what will he think of me? Some wanton woman, a sex-starved romance writer who lures men into her home under the guise of accepting food.

I'm a skank!

I finished the hamburger and set the plate aside. I

glanced down at the glob of ketchup on my fingers. "*Ah,* I need a napkin for—"

"Wait." Drew grasped my hand.

"But I—"

"Allow me."

"Allow you to wha—"

I gasped when he leaned forward and stuck out his tongue, licking the ketchup from my fingers, one by one.

My face heated, then my neck and chest. The warmth kept spreading south. Oh boy...

I tried to pull my hand back when I thought he was done, but Drew shook his head. He pulled me close. "You still have a little bit of ketchup left."

"Do I?" I wiggled my fingers.

"Not there." He angled his head toward mine and stuck out the tip of his tongue, running it around the left corner of my lips.

Holy cow...

He sat back and studied me. What was he doing? *He can't stop now.* I gazed into his eyes. Drew shrugged. "I got all the ketchup off. Was there...something else you needed?"

*Yeah...*I didn't speak, but desire must have shown in my eyes. With a smile, Drew put his hands on the sides of my face and pressed his lips to mine.

Ah yes...much better than chocolate. Or a hamburger.

Chapter Nine
Drew

The screech came from Cora's yard. What now? I hurried out the back door, not bothering to put on shoes. Cora held Chubbs, who was halfway up her shoulder. "Cora? What's going—"

A loud bark stopped me. Where was my dog? Cora pointed down in front of her. *This can't be good.* I rushed to the fence.

"Drew, please do something about your mongrel."

"Hey, he's not a—"

She gingerly lifted up her bare foot. The brown goopy mess was spread across her sole.

Blueprint barked again, and Chubbs was now clinging to Cora's shoulder with all of his claws out. Not good.

I scaled the fenced and dropped to her side. "Blueprint. How did you get over here?"

"He jumped over the fence and chased my cat." Chubbs howled and pawed at Cora's hair as if it was a rope he could climb to escape dangers below.

"Jumped the fence? *My* fence?"

Cora scowled at the word *my*. "Yes."

"It's not possible."

"Listen..." She tapped her foot on the grass then grimaced when the dog doo squished between her toes. "*Ugh.*" She wiped her foot on the grass a few times. "It's not all coming off. Great."

"Sorry about the mess, but there's no way on this earth that my dog made it over the fence."

Cora tugged Chubbs from her shoulder, winced at the engaged claws, and glared at me. "Wanna tell me how else he got in here, then? Maybe he parachuted. Or borrowed a trampoline and leaped high enough in the air to fly over. You've got the fence squared off at your house and your shed. No other way he could get over here except jump."

I shook my head. Blueprint was lazy. He hardly ever moved beyond a waddle unless it was to his food dish. I'd never even seen him wag his tail with much exuberance, as if it required too much energy. "No. It couldn't have happened. You need to understand—"

"No. *You* need to understand. There is dog poop in my yard. And on my foot. *Again.* This is unacceptable. And he terrorized my cat."

"Your cat sits on my fence and taunts him. I've seen it, and I know you have too."

"That doesn't—"

"If my dog got into your yard on his own, which I still don't believe, then he was provoked."

"What?" Her mouth dropped open.

"You heard me. How fair is it to put all the blame on Blueprint when your obnoxious cat—"

She gasped. "Don't you dare talk about my precious—"

"Precious?" I laughed. "He's a frowning furball without a single redeeming quality."

"*Well!* Your stupid poop machine has a...a stupid *name.* Who calls a dog Blueprint?"

"An engineer, that's who. Don't tell me the irony was lost on the writer girl?"

Cora narrowed her eyes. "Now *that* was rotten."

I pointed downward. "What's rotten is the stench coming from your foot."

"Which came from your worthless dog."

"Who was provoked by your unrepentant cat."

She hopped toward me, keeping her soiled foot raised four inches from the grass. Chubbs snarled. "Unrepentant? You make it sound like Chubbs did it on purpose."

"Of course he did."

"He's just being a cat. That's what they do."

"Torment poor helpless dogs?"

"They like to sit on things. And stare at stuff."

I raised my eyebrows. "Wow. *Things* and *stuff*. Surely a writer could come up with something more eloquent that that."

"*Believe* me. I have all sorts of words I'd like to use right now, especially for you."

I grinned. "Aww. Aren't you sweet? Some words of love and affection perhaps?"

"More like words of disgust and repulsion."

"Yeah, I will admit that stepping in dog doo is repulsive."

"I was talking about *you*."

I widened my eyes in mock horror. "Surely you jest."

"I'm not jesting."

"Might try it sometime Cora. Humor can be fun."

"I'm fun. I...I can be fun."

"If you say so." I picked up my rotund dog and heaved him over the fence. He landed on all fours but turned his head and gave me a reproachful glare. I was sure I'd have to make it up to him later. And it wouldn't be pretty.

Cora set her cat on the grass. He looked straight at me and hissed then trotted to the back door of Cora's house and stared at it. Was he expecting it to open on its own?

"Listen, I—"

"Save it, engineer boy. You can deny it all you want, but you and I both know that there is only one way that dog got over my fence."

I opened my mouth to protest that it wasn't *her* fence, but she held up her hand, palm out and then hopped on her unblemished foot in the direction of her hose. She circled her arms in the air while attempting to keep her balance. One arm must have twirled faster than the other because she spun to one side and plopped on her hip in the grass. Impressive was the fact that her poopy foot still never touched the ground.

I let out a sigh and hurried to get the hose. Making sure I had the volume on low this time, I sprayed the offensive substance from her foot.

"Thanks." She still wouldn't meet my eye.

"Least I could do since it came from my dog."

"You're right about that. It was the *least* you could do."

If I had any hope of getting closer to Cora, the arguing had to stop. Now. "Listen, I'm sorry about Blueprint. You're right that there's only one way he could have gotten over here." I darted a glance to the right and then back. "Although...he was trying to hide something from me when I walked into the garage the other day."

"He was?" She tilted her head.

I leaned closer, my lips brushing her hair when I whispered, "I'm fairly certain it was a pink parachute."

Cora snorted. "Pink? Quite the manly dog you have there."

"He loves pretty colors. He wanted to try on your strawberry bra, but I told him to restrain himself."

She shook her head slowly. "Aww, does Blueprint need some chest support?"

"Unfortunately. He's quite embarrassed about his doggy boobs."

"Don't you mean doobs?"

"Nice, Cora, making sport of my dog's plight."

She placed her hand on my arm. "I'm sorry. How thoughtless of me. If he truly needs help, I'll be glad to let him borrow one of mine. As long as he doesn't stretch it out." She snickered.

I glanced back at my dog. He glared at me and started licking his paw. "Actually, I'd say he *is* a little..."

"What?"

I whispered again. "Buxom."

Cora giggled. "I wouldn't know about being buxom, but I hear it can be quite the problem."

I glanced down at her chest, covered with a bright pink tank top. "I don't know. Looks pretty good to me."

Cora's skin reddened from her forehead to her chest.

Wouldn't it be wonderful to see if she was also blushing under her tank top on her—

"Well, I suppose I should get up. Can't spend the entire day lollygagging in the grass."

I put my hand on her arm, stopping her. She opened her eyes wide, and her gaze met mine and then lowered to my mouth. I edged closer. "What's wrong with lollygagging? Sounds like fun to me."

"I suppose it could be, if you're in the right company."

"Hmmm. Maybe we should experiment with what all can be done on the lawn."

She lifted one eyebrow and smiled. "You think?"

"Oh yeah." I slipped my hand behind her back and started to lower her. Cora's eyes drifted shut before I remembered something. "Wait."

Her eyes snapped open. "Wait?"

I eyed the ground surrounding us. "Wanted to make sure Blueprint hadn't left any other unwanted gifts."

"Good plan."

"Hey, I'm an engineer. We're great at plans."

She peeked over her shoulder. "All clear?"

"Yep. Now where were we?"

"Trying to discover one hundred and two ways to enjoy my yard."

"Only one hundred and two?"

"I'm open for new ideas."

My blood heated. "Good to know." I lowered her back down into the grass.

"I hate that we've been arguing, Drew."

"Me too." I ran tiny kisses down her neck.

"'Cause it seems to me that we like each other. I mean, I am lying in the grass with you. Can't say I've ever done that with anyone before."

"Neither have I." I ran my tongue beneath her ear and she shivered.

"I'm not sure where all this is headed."

I knew where I *wanted* it to go. "Anywhere you like, Cora."

She wrapped her arms around my neck. "You mean it?"

I smiled against her hair. "Of course."

"So, if I wanted us to date. That's what we'd do?"

"Isn't that what we're doing?"

"This is more like making out."

"But isn't it fun?" I pressed my lips to hers.

She pulled me closer until I was nearly on top of her. She giggled. "Yeah. I've actually thought a lot about doing this. With you."

"This? In the grass?"

"Maybe not in the grass." She ran her finger from my temple to my chin. Then she kissed the same path with her warm lips.

"Mmm. Then what have you—" I kissed her again. "—thought about?"

"You. Me...us."

Us? I leaned away. "You have?"

She turned her head away. "Um, yeah."

"Since when?"

Cora shrugged. "Since...always?"

*Always...*Was it possible that she'd been watching me the whole time I'd been watching her? And neither of us had been brave enough to do anything about it until now?

Cora turned her head. "Um... Shouldn't have said that."

I placed my finger beneath her chin, turning her head toward me. "Why not?"

"That's the kind of talk that scares guys away."

"Maybe not all guys."

"No?"

I shook my head and moved next to her, raised up on my elbow with my head on my hand. I leaned down and kissed her gently, then I angled my head and applied more pressure. Cora let out a little squeak when I rubbed my palm across her stomach. She reached up and ran her fingers though my hair at the nape of my neck. Desire shot straight through me.

She pulled away. "You know, it might not be such a great idea to do this out in my yard in broad daylight. Maybe we should stop."

A bucket of ice couldn't have cooled me off so fast. "Stop? Well, if that's what you want."

"It really isn't, but aside from that, I forgot one of the reasons why I never lay in the grass."

"Why? Grass stains on your clothes?"

"No. Chiggers." She edged out from under me and stood. Her whole body wiggled to a tune I couldn't hear as she scratched her arms and legs. "Ah! I've got to go take a shower."

I sat up. "Need help with that? The shower, I mean."

"No. You be *good*, Drew."

"If I must."

Cora frowned. "I'm going to run to the drug store for anti-itch medicine too. I'll need that after the shower." She eyed me. "The shower I'll take by myself." She walked a few steps and stopped. "Shoot."

"What?"

"I have *no* food. I'd better hit the grocery too." She waved. "Not sure when I'll be back."

"I'm not going anywhere."

She winked and left.

Cora went inside and closed her back door. After she was gone, I eyed the fence. The cause of the arguments. The unfortunate choice I'd made not all that long ago when I thought, *Hey wouldn't a wooden fence be cool right here?* Now that she and I were getting closer, I didn't want anything to spoil it. No more quarrels. Only getting along. And kissing. Lots and lots of kissing.

Before I could talk myself out of it, I went into the house and put on sturdy shoes. Then I rummaged around in the garage for the tool I needed and returned to the fence.

As much as I hated to do it, my actions were necessary if I wanted to keep a good relationship with Cora going.

I raised the axe and swung downward in a perfect arc. The wood splintered, pieces flying in all directions. I'd spent so many hours and a lot of money on the fence, but at the moment, none of that mattered. If it was going to cause problems between me and Cora, then it wasn't worth the wood it was made of.

I swung again, cracking a cross beam from a post. My shoulders protested the shock my body absorbed when metal collided with wood, but I felt free. Liberated. Maybe I'd put up too many fences in my life. Trying to keep out the possibility of getting hurt.

I chopped away at a lower rung, chunks of wood

thumping against the ground.

Had I closed myself in so tightly that I hadn't noticed that the girl I liked, liked me back? Well, no more. No more fences made of wood or thought. From now on, I'd stay open to new possibilities. Throw apprehension out the door and welcome change and possible love.

But could I really do that? Change what was the essence of me? Become a new man?

Probably not all at once, but working on the fence was a good start.

CHAPTER TEN
Cora

As I worked the soap over my skin, I shivered, remembering Drew's kisses, his touches and caresses. It hardly seemed possible that he was interested. In *me*. How many times had I sat in my room, mooning over his picture in the yearbook, just wishing he would notice me?

After I dried off, I liberally coated my arms and legs with lotion. Maybe that would help the itching until I could get the cream. Thank goodness it didn't smell like three-week-old tomatoes in July. I sniffed my arm. Green Apple. Yeah, I could deal with that. I knew Drew appreciated fruit, since he was taken with my fruit salad-colored bras on the fence. I giggled.

I dressed in a red halter top and white shorts. Usually I was covered more than that but figured it wouldn't hurt to keep him interested. What good were a girl's assets if she couldn't use them on the guy she'd liked forever?

When I got back home from shopping, I shoved my milk and yogurt in the fridge and set the rest of my purchases on the counter. The itching was still driving me crazy, so I dug the cream out of the bag and dabbed it on my bites. A knock sounded on the front door. I rushed toward it, nearly tripping over Chubbs, who sat directly in my path.

When I opened the door, Drew stood on the other side. "Hey."

"Hey, yourself."

"I've got something to show you."

He'd changed clothes too. A different shirt and shorts. And his hair was wet. Had he showered?

"Okay."

He reached out for my hand and led me around to my backyard.

"What do you—"

Drew shook his head. "Just wait."

"I'm not good at waiting."

"It's just back here, I promise."

When we rounded the corner, I gasped. "What happened to the fence?"

The middle section had been demolished; only a few partial posts still stood. It looked like a giant had stepped on it, crushing the wood to bits.

Drew led me to a green blanket that was spread over the grass beside the fence. When had that gotten there? How sweet that he was trying to keep any more chiggers from getting me.

"Cora, let me tell you a little story."

"An engineer? With a story? It's not about steel girders and hammers, is it?"

He laughed. "No. This is a story about a boy and a girl." We settled down on the blanket, sitting next to each other.

"That sounds more interesting. So what happens to them?" I laced my fingers through Drew's.

"The boy lived next to the cutest girl ever."

"Did he?"

"The *cutest*. He watched her when she was in her yard and wished she would come over to visit."

"But she didn't visit?"

"Not very often. It made the boy very sad."

"Why didn't he invite her? She might have gone

more."

"He was too shy."

"Shy? Are you sure?"

Drew nodded. "Extremely shy."

"That's too bad." I leaned closer.

"Yeah, it really was. Cause more than anything, he wanted to be her best friend."

"Aww that's sweet." A smile played on my lips.

"Then when the girl and the boy got older, he sat next to her in class every day for four years."

"Wow, that's a long time."

"Very long. And by then, he was dating another girl. One he thought was special, but who turned out not to be a very nice person."

"Oh."

"Also, the boy would see the girl with her friends. The ones who were into music, art, and books. He didn't think she would ever be interested in him anyway, because he was boring."

"Boring? No. The boy wasn't in the chess club, was he?" I poked Drew in the ribs.

"Unfortunately, he was their star member. See, he felt he had no chance with someone like her so he stayed with the other girl, the one who was only interested in having a boyfriend. Any boyfriend."

"But perhaps the boy was wrong."

"Wrong?"

"Maybe the girl didn't care if the boy was different from her. It could be that she found him cute and funny and interesting." I ran my finger down the side of Drew's neck.

"You think so?"

"Uh-huh. Maybe she even wished that when he was telling funny stories in class, he would include her in the fun."

Drew briefly pressed his forehead against mine. "The thing is, sometimes he told funny stories to get *her* attention."

"You did—I mean...*he* did?"

"Definitely."

"So...what happened to this boy and girl, after high school, when they grew up?"

"It's the funniest thing."

"Well the boy is *funny*, after all." I grinned.

"Right. So I've heard." Drew chuckled. "So they end up living next door to each other again. Same houses, moved in about the same time."

"Wow. What are the odds of that?"

"I would say minuscule at best."

"And what happened to them when they were neighbors again?" My fingers left Drew's neck and charted a course down his chest.

"When the girl moved in, she saw that the boy had built a fence."

"Ah. A fence. Pesky things they can be."

"He was sorry he'd built it. It caused them to argue and quarrel, which made the boy very sad."

I gazed at him and blinked. "I think maybe the girl was sad too."

"The boy knew how much the girl loved her cat, so he planned to do something for them. He was going to install a special, handmade scratching post to the fence at the exact point where the cat liked to sharpen his claws. The boy wondered if that would make the girl happy."

"I'm sure it would."

"And the boy decided that if the fence itself was evil, something had to be done. He used an axe and got rid of part of it."

"He did?" I brushed my hand over Drew's shoulder.

"Yep. He decided to put in a gate between their houses. Because anything that stood in the way of the boy and girl being friends wasn't worth it. The gate would open up their two yards to each other. Also...the gate would allow for new possibilities. Wonderful ones that the fence might not have allowed before. I think they decided to be friends after that. More than friends."

My mouth dropped open. "You *think*? You don't *know*?"

"The story is still being written, Cora."

I wrapped both arms around Drew's waist. "Would, perhaps, a romance writer be of some help with this story? I know of one who has a vested interest in the outcome."

"You know, I think she just might."

As Drew pressed his lips to mine, I decided that yes, I knew exactly how I wanted our story to end. Marriage. Family. A cute little house painted white with black shudders and lots and lots of flowers in the yard.

And a picket fence—with a gate!

The End

If you enjoyed *Over A Fence*, I would appreciate it if you'd help others enjoy it too!

Recommend it! Please help other readers find this book by recommending it to family, friends, readers' groups, libraries, and discussion boards.

Review it! The best way to support an author is to leave a review. Please take a minute to review *Over A Fence!*

Wanna make sure you don't miss the next esKape Press release? Just sign up for the esKape Press Newsletter at www.eskapepress.com. We only send the newsletter informing readers about new releases!

Thank you again and happy reading!

About the Author

Bestselling author Ruth J. Hartman spends her days herding cats and her nights spinning sweet romantic tales that make you smile, giggle, or laugh out loud. She, her husband, and their three cats love to spend time curled up in their recliners watching old Cary Grant movies. Well, the cats, Maxwell, Roxy, and Remmie, sit in the people's recliners. Not that the cats couldn't get their own furniture. They just choose to shed on someone else's. You know how selfish those little furry creatures can be.

Ruth, a left-handed, cat-herding, Jeep driving, farmhouse-dwelling romance writer uses her goofy sense of humor as she writes tales of lovable, klutzy women and the men who adore them. Ruth's husband and best friend, Garry, reads her manuscripts, rolls his eyes at her weird story ideas, and loves her in spite of her penchant for insisting all of her books have at least one cat in them. Or twelve. But hey, who's counting?

www.ruthjhartman.blogspot.com
www.facebook.com/ruth.j.hartman
www.twitter.com/RuthjHartman
www.goodreads.com/author/show/3312900.Ruth_J_Hartman

esKape Press

**Any time...
Any place...
Any day...
Getaway.**

www.eskapepress.com